CALL IT
COURAGE

CALL IT COURAGE

Armstrong Sperry

Illustrations by the Author

Aladdin Paperbacks

Aladdin Paperbacks
An imprint of Simon & Schuster
Children's Publishing Division
1230 Avenue of the Americas
New York, NY 10020
Copyright © 1940 by Simon & Schuster, Inc.
Copyright renewed 1968 by Armstrong Perry.
All rights reserved including the right of reproduction in whole or in part in any form.
First Aladdin Paperbacks edition, 1990
First Collier Books edition, 1971
Also available in a hardcover edition from
Simon & Schuster Books for Young Readers.
Manufactured in the United States of America
10 9 8 7 6 5 4 3 2 1

Library of Congress Cataloging-in-Publication Data
Sperry, Armstrong, 1897–1976
Call it courage/Armstrong Sperry.—50th anniversary ed., 1st
Aladdin Books ed.
     p.   cm.
Summary: Relates how Mafatu, a young Polynesian boy whose name means Stout Heart, overcomes his terrible fear of the sea and proves his courage to himself and his people.
ISBN 0-689-71391-6
[1. Folklore—Polynesia.   2. Courage—Folklore.   3. Survival—Folklore.]   I. Title.
PZ8.1.S75Cal   1990
398.2—dc20   89-18456 CIP AC
ISBN 0-689-86229-6

CONTENTS

1. FLIGHT

I T HAPPENED many years ago, before the traders and missionaries first came into the South Seas, while the Polynesians were still great in numbers and fierce of heart. But even today the people of Hikueru sing this story in their chants and tell it over the evening fires. It is the story of Mafatu, the Boy Who Was Afraid.

They worshiped courage, those early Polynesians. The spirit which had urged them across the Pacific in their sailing canoes, before the dawn of recorded history, not knowing where they were going nor caring what their fate might be, still sang its song of danger in their blood. There was only courage. A man who was afraid—what place had he in their midst? And the boy Mafatu—son of Tavana Nui, the Great Chief of Hikueru—always had been afraid. So the people drove him forth. Not by violence, but by indifference.

Mafatu went out alone to face the thing he feared the most. And the people of Hikueru still sing his story in their chants and tell it over the evening fires.

It was the sea that Mafatu feared. He had been surrounded by it ever since he was born. The thunder of it filled his ears; the crash of it upon the reef, the mutter of it at sunset, the threat and fury of its storms—on every hand, wherever he turned—the sea.

He could not remember when the fear of it first had taken hold of him. Perhaps it was during the great hurricane which swept Hikueru when he was a child of three. Even now, twelve years later, Mafatu could remember that terrible morning. His mother had taken him out to the barrier-reef to search for sea urchins in the reef pools. There were other canoes scattered at wide intervals along the reef. With late afternoon the other fishermen began to turn back. They shouted warnings to Mafatu's mother. It was the season of hurricane and the people of Hikueru were nervous and ill at ease, charged, it seemed, with an almost animal awareness of impending storm.

But when at last Mafatu's mother turned back toward shore, a swift current had set in around the shoulder of the reef-passage: a meeting of tides that swept like a millrace out into the open sea. It seized the frail craft in its swift race. Despite all the woman's skill, the canoe was carried on the crest of the churning tide, through the reef-passage, into the outer ocean.

Mafatu would never forget the sound of his mother's despairing cry. He didn't know then what it meant; but he felt that something was terribly wrong, and he set up a loud wailing. Night closed down upon them, swift as a frigate's wing, darkening the known world. The wind of the open ocean rushed in at them, screaming. Waves lifted and struck at one another, their crests hissing with spray. The poles of the outrigger were torn from their thwarts. The woman sprang forward to seize her child as the canoe capsized. The little boy gasped when the cold water struck him. He clung to his mother's neck. Moana, the Sea God, was reaching up for them, seeking to draw them down to his dark heart. . . .

Off the tip of Hikueru, the uninhabited islet of Tekoto lay shrouded in darkness. It was scarcely more than a ledge of coral, almost awash. The swift current bore directly down upon the islet.

Dawn found the woman still clinging to the *purau* pole and the little boy with his arms locked about his mother's neck. The grim light revealed sharks circling, circling. . . . Little Mafatu buried his head against his mother's cold

9

neck. He was filled with terror. He even forgot the thirst that burned his throat. But the palms of Tekoto beckoned with their promise of life, and the woman fought on.

When at last they were cast up on the pinnacle of coral, Mafatu's mother crawled ashore with scarcely enough strength left to pull her child beyond reach of the sea's hungry fingers. The little boy was too weak even to cry. At hand lay a cracked coconut; the woman managed to press the cool, sustaining meat to her child's lips before she died.

Sometimes now, in the hush of night, when the moon was full and its light lay in silver bands across the pandanus mats, and all the village was sleeping, Mafatu awoke and sat upright. The sea muttered its eternal threat to the reef. The sea. . . . And a terrible trembling seized the boy's limbs, while a cold sweat broke out on his forehead. Mafatu seemed to see again the faces of the fishermen who had found the dead mother and her whimpering child. These pictures still colored his dreams. And so it was that he shuddered when the mighty seas, gathering far out, hurled themselves at the barrier-reef of Hikueru and the whole island quivered under the assault.

Perhaps that was the beginning of it. Mafatu, the boy who had been christened Stout Heart by his proud father, was afraid of the sea. What manner of fisherman would he grow up to be? How would he ever lead the men in battle against warriors of other islands? Mafatu's father heard the whispers, and the man grew silent and grim.

The older people were not unkind to the boy, for they believed that it was all the fault of the *tupapau*—the ghost-spirit which possesses every child at birth. But the girls laughed at him, and the boys failed to include him in their games. And the voice of the reef seemed pitched for his ears alone; it seemed to say: "You cheated me once, Mafatu, but someday, someday I will claim you!"

Mafatu's stepmother knew small sympathy for him, and his stepbrothers treated him with open scorn.

"Listen," they would mock. "Moana, the Sea God, thunders on the reef. He is angry with us all because Mafatu is afraid!"

The boy learned to turn these jibes aside, but his father's silence shamed him. He tried with all his might to overcome his terror of the sea. Sometimes, steeling himself against it, he went with Tavana Nui and his stepbrothers out beyond the reef to fish. Out there, where the glassy swells of the ocean lifted and dropped the small canoe, pictures crowded into the boy's mind, setting his scalp atingle: pictures of himself, a babe, clinging to his mother's back . . . sharks cruising. . . . And so overcome would he be at the remembrance of that time that he would drop his spear overboard, or let the line go slack at the wrong moment and lose the fish.

It was obvious to everyone that Mafatu was useless upon the sea. He would never earn his proper place in the tribe. Stout Heart—how bitter the name must taste upon his father's lips!

So, finally, he was not allowed to fare forth with the fishermen. He brought ill luck. He had to stay at home making spears and nets, twisting coir—the husk of the coconut—into stout sharkline for other boys to use. He became very skillful at these pursuits, but he hated them. His heart was like a stone in his breast.

A nondescript yellow dog named Uri was Mafatu's inseparable companion—Uri with his thin coat which showed his ribs, and his eyes so puzzled and true. He followed the boy wherever he went. Their only other friend was Kivi, an albatross. The boy had once found the bird on his lonely wanderings. One of Kivi's feet was smaller than the other. Perhaps because it was different from its kind, the older birds were heckling and pestering the fledgling. Something about that small bird trying to fight off its more powerful fellows touched the boy's heart. He picked it up and carried it home—caught fish for it in the shallows of the lagoon. The bird followed Mafatu and Uri about, limping on its one good leg. At length, when the young albatross learned to fly, it began to find its own food. In the air it achieved perfection, floating serenely against the sky while Mafatu followed its effortless flight with envious eyes. If only he, too, could escape to some world far removed from Hikueru!

Now, once more, it was the beginning of the season of storms. Men scanned the skies anxiously, watching for the dreaded signs which might spell the destruction of their world. Soon the great bonitos would be swimming beyond

13

the reef—hundreds, thousands of them—for they came each year at this time with the unfailing regularity of the tides. They were held to be the special property of young boys, since it was by killing them that a youth learned to kill the swordfishes and tiger-sharks, progressing from one stage to a higher. Every boy in the village sharpened his spear, tested the shaft, honed his shark knife. Every boy, that is, except Mafatu.

Kana stopped one afternoon to watch Mafatu at work on his nets. Of all the youths of his own age, Kana alone had been friendly. Sometimes he even stayed behind when the others were fishing to help the boy with his work.

"The bonitos have begun to run, Mafatu," Kana said quietly.

"Yes," the other returned, then fell silent. His fingers faltered as they flew among the sennit fibers of the net he was making.

"My father brought back word from the reef today," Kana went on. "Already there are many bonitos out there. Tomorrow we boys will go after them. That's our job. It will be fun, eh?"

Mafatu's knuckles whitened. His ears pounded with the swift fury of the sea. . . .

"That will be fun, won't it?" Kana insisted, watching Mafatu closely. But the boy made no answer. Kana started to speak; he stopped, turned impatiently, and walked away. Mafatu wanted to cry out after him: "Wait, Kana! I'll go! I'll try—" But the words would not come. Kana had gone.

14

Tomorrow he and all the other boys would be taking their canoes out beyond the reef. They would return at sunset, loaded down with bonitos, their faces happy, their shouts filling the dusk. Their fathers would say: "See what a fine fisherman is my son! He will be a Chief one of these days." Only Tavana Nui would be silent. *His* son had not gone.

That night a new moon rose above the edge of the sea, silvering the land with a bloom of magic. Wandering along the outer beach with Uri, Mafatu heard laughing voices and drew hastily into the black shadow of a pandanus. A group of boys were pulling their canoes above high water-mark, and laying their plans for the morrow. Their voices were shrill with eagerness.

"Tomorrow at daybreak . . ." one was saying.

"There'll be Timi and Tapu and Viri . . ."

"*Aué!*" another voice broke in. "It's work for us all. How else will we become fishermen and warriors? How else will we feed our families and keep the tribe alive?"

"True! Hikueru is too poor. There are only the fish from the sea. A man must be fearless to provide food. We will all go—every one of us!"

Mafatu, standing tense in the shadows, heard a scornful laugh. His heart contracted. "Not all of us will go," he heard Kana scoff. "Not Mafatu!"

"Ha! He is afraid."

"He makes good spears," offered Viri generously.

"Ho! That is woman's work. Mafatu is afraid of the sea.

16

He will never be a warrior." Kana laughed again, and the scorn of his voice was like a spear thrust through Mafatu's heart. "*Aiá!*" Kana was saying. "I have tried to be friendly with him. But he is good only for making spears. Mafatu is a coward."

The boys disappeared down the moonlit beach. Their laughter floated back on the night air. Mafatu stood quite still. Kana had spoken; he had voiced, once for all, the feeling of the tribe. Mafatu—Stout Heart—was a coward. He was the Boy Who Was Afraid.

His hands were damp and cold. His nails dug into his palms. Suddenly a fierce resentment stormed through him. He knew in that instant what he must do: he must prove

17

his courage to himself, and to the others, or he could no longer live in their midst. He must face Moana, the Sea God—face him and conquer him. He must.

The boy stood there taut as a drawn arrow awaiting its release. Off to the south somewhere there were other islands. . . . He drew a deep breath. If he could win his way to a distant island, he could make a place for himself among strangers. And he would never return to Hikueru until he should have proven himself! He would come back with his head high-held in pride, and he would hear his father say: "Here is my son Stout Heart. A brave name for a brave boy." . . . Standing there with clenched fists, Mafatu knew a smarting on his eyelids and shut his eyes tight, and sank his teeth into his lower lip.

Far off in the *himené* house the Old Ones were singing. Their voices filled the night with rich sound. They sang of long voyages in open canoes, of hunger and thirst and battle. They sang the deeds of heroes. The hair on the boy's damp forehead stirred; the long-drawn mutter of the reef sounded its note of warning in his ears. At his side, Uri touched his master's hand with a cold nose. Mafatu pulled the dog close.

"We're going away, Uri," he whispered fiercely. "Off to the south there are other islands." . . .

The outrigger canoes lay drawn up on the beach like long slim fish. Silent as a shadow, the boy crossed the sand. His heart was hammering in his throat. Into the nearest canoe he flung half a dozen green drinking nuts, his fish spear. He gave his *pareu* a brave hitch. Then he picked up a paddle and called to Uri. The dog leaped into the bow. There was only Kivi—Mafatu would miss his albatross. He scanned the dark sky for sight of the bird, then gave it up and turned away.

The lagoon was as untroubled as a mirror. Upon its black face the stars lay tracks of fire. The boy shoved off and climbed into the stern. Noiselessly he propelled the canoe forward, sending it half a length ahead with each thrust of his paddle. As he drew nearer to the barrier-reef, the thunder of the surf increased. The old, familiar dread of it struck at his stomach's pit, and made him falter in his paddling. The voices of the Old Ones were fainter and fainter now.

The reef thunder mounted: a long-drawn, hushed yet mighty sound that seemed to have its being not in the air above but in the very sea beneath. Out beyond lurked a terrifying world of water and wind. Out there lay everything most to be feared. The boy's hands tightened on his paddle. Behind him lay safety, security from the sea. What matter if they jeered? For a second he almost turned back. Then he heard Kana's voice once more saying: "Mafatu is a coward."

The canoe entered the race formed by the ebbing tide. It caught up the small craft in its churn, swept it forward like a chip on a millrace. No turning back now. . . .

The boy was aware of a sudden whir and fury in the sky above, a beat of mighty wings. Startled, he glanced upward. There was Kivi, his albatross. Mafatu's heart lifted. The bird circled slowly in the moonlight, its wings edged with silver. It hovered for a moment just over the bow of the canoe, then it rose easily, lightly in its effortless flight. Out through the passage in the reef. Out into the open ocean.

Mafatu gripped the steering paddle and followed.

2. THE SEA

DAY broke over a gray and dismal world. The canoe lifted and fell idly on the glassy swells. Mafatu looked back over his shoulder, searching the horizon for a last glimpse of Hikueru; but the atoll had vanished, as if to hide itself forever from his concern.

The matting sail slatted uselessly. But there seemed to be no need of a sail: the little canoe was riding one of the mysterious ocean currents that flow in their courses through the length and breadth of the Pacific: the *Ara Moana,* Paths of the Sea, as the Ancients called them. They were

the ocean currents that had carried the Polynesian navi-
gators from island to island in the childhood of the world.
Mafatu was drifting farther and farther away from his
homeland.

With wide-flapping wings Kivi rose from the bow of the
canoe. In ascending spirals the bird climbed higher and
higher, until at last he was no more than a gray speck
against the lighter gray of the sky. Mafatu watched his
albatross disappear and felt a desolation flood his heart.
Now there was only Uri to keep him company in this hostile
world of sky and sea. Uri. . . . The yellow dog lay curled
up in the shadow of the bow, opening one eye from time
to time to look at his master. Wherever Mafatu went, Uri,
too, would go.

All around, as far as the eye could reach, were wastes
of leaden water. The canoe was the moving center of a
limitless circle of sea. The boy shuddered. His fingers
gripped the paddle convulsively. He thought of Kana and
the other boys—what would they say when they learned
that he had disappeared? And Tavana Nui—would there
be sorrow in his father's heart? Would he believe that
Moana, the Sea God, had claimed his son at last?

It was an ominous, oppressive world at this season of
storm. Half a mile distant a whale heaved its varnished
hulk to the surface, to throw a jet of vapory mist high into
the air; then it submerged, leaving scarcely a ripple to
mark its passage. A shoal of flying fishes broke water,

skimming away in a silver shimmer of flight. A dolphin sped after them, smooth-rolling in pursuit, so close that the boy could hear the sound of its breathing. This world of the sea was ruled by Nature's harsh law of survival. Mafatu knew the sea with an intimacy given to few. He had seen fleets of giant mantas whipping the lagoon of Hikueru to a boiling fury; he had seen the mighty cachalot set upon by killer-whales and torn to ribbons almost in the blink of an eye; once he had seen an octopus as large as the trunk of a tamanu, with tentacles thirty feet long, rise from the mile-deep water beyond the barrier-reef. . . . *Ai*, this sea!

Mafatu opened one of the green drinking nuts and tilted back his head to let the cool liquid trickle down his parched throat; more refreshing than spring water, cool on the hottest days, and as sustaining as food. The boy scooped out the gelatinous meat for Uri and the dog ate it gratefully.

The ocean current which held the canoe in its grip seemed to have quickened. There was a wind rising, too, in little puffs and gusts. Now the canoe heeled over under the sudden attack, while Mafatu scrambled onto the outrigger to lend his weight for ballast; then the wind dropped as suddenly as it appeared, while the canoe righted itself and the boy breathed freely once again. He searched the skies for Kivi. His albatross might have been one of a thousand sea birds flying against the roof of the sky, or he might have vanished utterly, leaving his friends here in solitary space. The bird had led Mafatu out through the reef-passage at Hikueru into the open ocean, and now, it seemed, had deserted him.

A storm was making, moving in out of those mysterious belts which lie north and south of the equator, the home of hurricanes. The wind shifted a point, bringing with it a heavy squall. Mafatu lowered the sail on the run and gripped the steering paddle with hands that showed white at the knuckles. All around him now was a world of tumbling water, gray in the hollows, greenish on the slopes. The wind tore off the combing crests and flung the spray at the sky. Like advance scouts of an oncoming army, wind gusts moved down upon the canoe, struck at it savagely. So busy was Mafatu with the paddle that there was no time for thought. He called a prayer to Maui, God of the Fishermen:

"Maui é! E matai tu!"

Somehow the sound of his own voice reassured him. Uri lifted his head, cocked his ears, thumped his tail for a second. The canoe rose to the swells as lightly as a gull and coasted like a sled down the frothing slopes. What skill had wrought this small canoe! This dugout, hewn from the mighty tamanu tree. It swooped and yielded, bucked and scudded, one with the fierce element whose back it rode.

The sky darkened. A burst of lightning lit up the sea with supernatural brilliance. An instantaneous crack of thunder shattered the world. Lightning again, striking at the hissing water. Mafatu watched it with fascinated eyes.

24

Now it was all about him. It ran to the end of the boom in globes of fire that exploded and vanished, and in the awful moment of its being it revealed mountain shapes of dark water, heaving, shouldering. . . . How long could this frail craft of wood and sennit resist? Under the combined attack of wind and sea it seemed that something must inevitably give way. The wind shrilled a fiercer note. Spray stung the boy's flesh, blinded his eyes, chilled his marrow.

The sail went first—with a split and a roar. Fragments swept off on the back of the wind. The cords that held the mast hummed like plucked wires. Then with a rending groan the mast cracked. Before Mafatu could leap to cut it clear, it snapped off and disappeared in a churn of black water. The boy clung to the paddle, fighting to keep his canoe from turning broadside. Water swept aboard and out again. Only the buoyancy of tamanu kept the craft afloat. Uri cowered in the bow, half submerged, his howls drowned by the roar of the elements. Mafatu gripped his paddle for very life, an unreasoning terror powering his arms. This sea that he had always feared was rising to claim him, just as it had claimed his mother. How rightly he had feared it! Moana, the Sea God, had been biding his time. . . . "Someday, Mafatu, I will claim you!"

The boy lost all sense of time's passage. Every nerve became dulled by tumult. The wind howled above his head and still Mafatu clung to the lashed steering paddle; clung fast long after strength had vanished and only the will to live locked his strong fingers about the shaft. Even death

26

would not loose the grip of those fingers. He held his little craft true to the wind.

There was a wave lifting before the canoe. Many the boy had seen, but this was a giant—a monster livid and hungry. Higher, higher it rose, until it seemed that it must scrape at the low-hanging clouds. Its crest heaved over with a vast sigh. The boy saw it coming. He tried to cry out. No sound issued from his throat. Suddenly the wave was upon him. Down it crashed. *Chaos!* Mafatu felt the paddle torn from his hands. Thunder in his ears. Water strangling him. Terror in his soul. The canoe slewed round into the trough. The boy flung himself forward, wound his arms about the mid-thwart. It was the end of a world.

The wave passed. Stunned, gasping, Mafatu raised his head and looked about. For a second he could not believe that he still breathed and had being. He saw Uri wedged under the bow, choking for air. He pulled the dog free. Then he saw that his string of drinking nuts had vanished. His fish spear was gone. The knife that hung about his neck by a twist of bark had been torn away. Even his *pareu* of fiber tapa fell from his body as water soaked it through. He was naked, defenseless, without food or weapon, hurled forward on the breath of the hurricane. Numb of all feeling, empty as a shell, still he clung to life, and the hours droned by. . . .

So gradual was the storm's easing that at first the boy was unaware of it. The wind was blowing itself out, moving off into the empty spaces of the world. Uri crept toward

27

the prostrate boy, quailing beside him, whimpering softly.
Night came and passed.

There was no morning mist to dim the splendor of the
sunburst across the swinging seas. Far away the wings
of an albatross caught its gold as it wheeled and planed
against the roof of heaven. The only hint of recent storm
lay in the rough and tumbling waters. As the sun climbed
through the hot hours of morning, it burned into the boy's
body like the sacred fires of the great marae of Hikueru.
Mafatu's skin blistered and cracked. His tongue swelled
in his throat. He tried to call out a prayer to Maui, but his
voice was thick; the sounds which came forth were no more
than a hoarse cry. The canoe, stripped of sail and mast,
without a paddle to guide it in the swift-racing current,
twisted and shifted in the rushing waters.

As one hour merged into another there came moments of
fitful, choking slumber, a growing agony of thirst for the
boy and his dog. The sun burned into them like an inescap-
able eye. The current which held Mafatu's canoe fast in
its grip was bearing it swiftly on toward its mysterious
destination.

And thus the day passed, while night once more descended, bringing blessed release from the sun.

Now the air was luminous with promise of another day.
Out of the sultry mists the sea emerged, blue and violent.
With the coming of this new day terror raised its head.

Mafatu tried to fight it back, to deny its existence; but it gripped his heart with clammy fingers, tightened his throat. He flung himself flat on the floor of the canoe and buried his face in his arms. He must have cried out then. His voice was but a hoarse croak, yet it stirred Uri to life: the dog's ragged tail gave one feeble thump. With the ghost of a whimper the animal laid his hot nose against the boy's hand.

The brave thump of his dog's tail touched Mafatu profoundly. He caught the animal to him, while a new assurance, a new strength, flooded his being. If Uri could have courage to die, surely he, Mafatu, could not do less! In that instant he heard a whir and fury in the sky above, a beat of wide wings. . . . Looking upward, the boy's dulled eyes made out the widespread wings of an albatross, circling above the canoe.

"Kivi!" Mafatu cried hoarsely. "*Ai*, Kivi!"

Even as he spoke, the bird wheeled slowly, then flew off straight ahead for the distant horizon. The boy noticed then that the sea current was carrying him almost due southwest. Kivi's flight moved in exact parallel. Once more it seemed as if his albatross were leading him onward, just as he had led the canoe out of the passage of Hikueru.

Mafatu scanned the rim of the horizon; it looked as hard as the cut edge of a stone. But suddenly the boy's heart gave a great leap and he started forward. *It couldn't be!* It was a cloud. . . . But the sky was cloudless. Far off in the sea-shimmer lay something that was neither sea nor sky. The swells, lifting higher, now revealed, now concealed it. That shadow on the horizon—it was land! The boy flung himself forward, shaking uncontrollably.

He seized Uri in his arms and lifted him up, laughing, crying: "Uri! Uri! It's land. *Land!*"

The dog sniffed at the air and a little whimper broke from him.

What island could this be? Was it Tahiti, the golden island, whose language was akin to that of Hikueru? Or was it, perhaps, one of the terrible dark islands of the eaters-of-men?

Now the current had a westward drift, and it was to the west that the dark islands lay. . . .

All day, as the canoe drifted onward, the boy watched
the distant shadow-shape of land, not daring to take his
eyes from it lest it vanish into the sea. Hunger and thirst
were lulled into forgetfulness. There was only this one
reality, land—escape from the sea. Weak as he was, he still
clung to the thwart, his lips whispering a silent prayer of
gratitude. With waning afternoon, the island took more
distinct form as the canoe drifted nearer. It was high and
peaked, its valleys blue-shadowed against the paler tone
of the sky. Hour by hour, with every lift of the swells, the
island rose higher and higher, filling Mafatu's soul with
wonder. Hikueru, the only land he had ever seen, was as
flat as his hand; but a great single peak crowned this
strange island. Trees rose green and fair, tier upon tier of
them, from the shoreline into the foothills of the purple
mountain. Uri had caught the scent of the land now and
was quivering with delight.

Then from far off came the first muffled thunder of the
reef: the boom of the surf high-bursting on the barrier
coral. That sound—was it the voice of Moana? "Someday,
Mafatu, someday." . . . Involuntarily the boy shuddered.
Would his ears never be free of the Sea God's threat?

Mafatu was powerless to guide his craft. He sensed that
the current had quickened. He could only watch helplessly
as the little canoe, swift as the following gulls, rushed to
meet the tides of the island where they met and churned
in a cross sea of conflict. Now across the swells came a
sound like a chorus of ghostly fishermen weary with their

day's toil: sea birds, always complaining, never at rest; while softer, yet rising above it was another sound—the voice of the reef itself, quieting with sundown, like the reassuring hush of a mother to her child.

Night stole up from the face of the sea, enveloping the world. There was no moon, but the black sky was spangled with unguessed millions of stars: other worlds, other suns. To the watching boy, with land in the offing, they seemed closer and more friendly. The bottom star of the Southern Cross pointed to the end of the world. . . . A soft land breeze, heavy with a scent of flowers, wafted out across the dark waters, tantalizing, bitter-sweet.

Weak with thirst, the boy drifted now into a merciful sleep. He struggled against it, like a weary swimmer fighting a rip-tide, but his head drooped and his eyes closed.

He was aroused at midnight by a thunderous tumult in his ears. Of a sudden he felt the canoe under him lifted and flung high into the air. Then down it crashed into splinters upon the reef. Boy and dog were hurled headlong into the boiling surf.

The shock of cold water brought Mafatu half back to consciousness. Blindly he struck out, fighting for survival. Uri—where was he? No sign of the dog. The boy was aware that the canoe must have been flung over the barrier-reef, for here the water was scarcely troubled by wind or tide. Now he was swimming, swimming. . . . Somewhere ahead a strip of beach, salt-white in the darkness, lured him onward. His muscles did it of themselves. Only a will to live.

A strip of sand white in the night. . . . He caught the gleam of a shark's belly, close at hand, but on he swam. His unhampered limbs moved freely through the water.

Of a sudden there was something solid beneath his feet. Sand. Mafatu stumbled, staggered, fell to his knees in the shallows. His lips moved in dry, soundless speech. Lying there with the water rippling and breaking over him, he pulled himself half upright, swayed onward. The palms, trooping to the edge of the beach, were motionless in the night air. All the world seemed to hold its breath as this boy climbed up out of the sea.

He fell to the sand once more, then, guided by he knew not what impulse, he dragged himself to the edge of the jungle. A murmur of water reached his ears, soft as a chuckle of pleasant laughter. Water, sweet water. . . . Down the face of an age-worn rock a small cascade lost itself amid ferns and cool mosses. A ragged, strangling cry broke from Mafatu's throat. He stood upright to full height. Then he crashed to the mossy bank. One cheek lay in the cool water.

The moon lifted above the rim of the palms. It outlined in silver the form of a boy thin with hunger, naked as the daystar. It revealed a small wet dog, dragging himself across the beach to his master's side.

Mafatu lay without moving. Before Uri drank, he touched the boy's cheek with his hot muzzle.

3. THE ISLAND

THERE was a fan of light spreading in the east. Mafatu stirred and opened his eyes. For a moment he lay there motionless in the cool mosses, forgetful of the events which had cast him up on this strange shore. Then it all came crowding back upon him, and he scarcely dared to believe that there was earth, solid earth beneath him; that once more Moana, the Sea God, had been cheated. He struggled to sit upright, then fell back upon one elbow. Uri lay close at hand, holding a robber-crab in his forepaws, cracking the tough shell and extracting the meat with gusto. There was Kivi, too, with his beak tucked back under his wing in sleep. Kivi, who had led his friends to this island. . . .

Mafatu pulled himself to a sitting position. The action called for more strength than he realized. He was giddy with thirst and there was an odd weakness in his limbs. His right leg was swollen and painful. He remembered then that he had banged it against the coral when the canoe struck. He discovered that there was a gash on his calf; he must take care of it, for coral wounds were poisonous.

The chuckle of the cascade reached his ears and made him aware of a stabbing need of water. He plunged his face into the pool and drank deeply. Then, prompted more by instinct than by conscious thought, he withdrew, to let the water run down his swollen throat sparingly, with caution. Its cool magic stole through his tissues, bringing with it new life and restoring force. He sighed, and sank back on the mossy bank, relishing the strength that quickened his tired body. Soon he must find food. . . . There were thousands of coconut trees on every hand, rich with green fruit; but Mafatu was not yet strong enough to climb. Later he would try it. Then he would make fire, too; and he must search the island to find out if it were inhabited; and there was a shelter to build. Oh, there was much to do! He hardly knew where to begin. But now it was enough just to lie there and feel strength returning, to know that he was safe from the sea. The sea. . . . He shuddered. Maui, God of the Fishermen, had carried him safely across the ocean currents.

"Uri," the boy muttered thickly, "we're alive! It wasn't all a bad dream. It really happened."

The answering wag of his dog's tail was further assurance of reality. As Mafatu's brain cleared of cobwebs, a sudden thought brought him up swiftly: this silent island was not Tahiti. What island was it then? Did it . . . oh! did it belong to the black eaters-of-men? Were they even now watching him from secret places in the jungle, biding their time? He glanced about in apprehension. But the solitude was unbroken save for the soft cooing of ghost-terns and the gentle plash of the cascade.

On his left hand, far offshore, the reef boomed to the charging surf; the curve of the beach reached out like two great arms to inclose the lagoon. Coconuts and pandanus trooped in shining legions to the very edge of the sea. A flight of green and purple parakeets flashed across the sky and vanished. There was no other sign of life. No voices of men; no laughter of children; no footprint in the sand.

The volcanic peak that formed the background of the island rose perhaps three thousand feet straight up out of the sea. It was the cone of a volcano long extinct. From its base ridges of congealed lava flowed down to the distant shore. Once, in the dim beginnings of the world, this mountain had belched forth fire and brimstone, spreading destruction over the land. But the forgiving jungle through fertile centuries had crept back up the slopes, clothing them in green, green.

The boy rose and stood stretching his stiff limbs. The water had restored him and he felt much stronger. But he found that the earth heaved with the sea's own motion, and he swayed to keep his balance. His leg still pained, and he would need the juice of limes to cauterize the coral wound, and *purau* leaves to make a healing bandage. Near by was a tree loaded with wild limes. He plucked half a dozen of the fruits, broke them on a bit of coral, and squeezed the juice into the wound. He winced as the caustic stung; but when he had bound on the leafy bandage with a twist of vine, it seemed that already his leg felt better. Soon the swelling would be gone.

Close at hand he discovered a rude trail made by wild pigs and goats in their wanderings across the mountain. The trail led up through the foothills to a high plateau which, the boy decided, would make a splendid lookout. From that point of vantage he would be able to survey his entire island and the sea for a distance of many miles.

He followed the path where it led back into the jungle, along the course of the swift-flowing stream. The trail sloped up sharply and Mafatu pulled himself up by roots and trailing lianas, now climbing, now crawling flat on his stomach. He found that he had to stop every now and then to catch his breath. Uri ran beside him, dashing off on this scent and that; the dog's shrill, sharp bark shattered the morning stillness.

For a quarter of a mile the coconuts held, beautiful trees that were more luxuriant than any in Hikueru. It was always thus in the rich soil of the volcanic islands. Then came a belt of breadfruit and wild bananas, of oranges and guavas and mangoes. The roots of the *mapé* trees—the island chestnut—twisted over the ground in strange, tormented shapes. Vines trailed like aerial ropes from the high branches where orchids bloomed, while little parakeets fled on swift wings and vanished in the green gloom. Mafatu had never before seen woods like these, for Hikueru was open and wind-swept. These endless legions of trees seemed to close in upon him, imprison him with reaching arms, with heady odors, with eerie light and shadow. Ferns grew higher than a tall man's head; the roof of leaves was powdered with starry blossoms.

By the time Mafatu reached the plateau he was exhausted and his leg throbbed with pain. He lay down full length upon the volcanic rock and watched wild goats leaping from peak to peak high above his head and heard their shrill bleating in the clear air. When he caught his breath he sat up again and looked about. The plateau appeared to divide the island into halves. From his vantage point the boy could see its whole circumference. He was hoping desperately for some sign of human habitation, yet fearing it too; for who knew whether humans might prove friends or enemies? He almost hoped that the island were uninhabited, but if it were— He shivered as he realized his isolation. Even at sea in his small canoe he had not felt so utterly alone as he did here on this strange, high island. Everything about it was alien and forbidding.

He stood there looking off to the southwest, and all at once his heart gave a jump, and he strained forward. A cone-shape, vague as a cloud upon the horizon, showed him the existence of another high island. It must have been fifty miles distant. As the boy watched eagerly, scarcely daring to believe the testimony of his eyes, he saw what might have been a column of smoke lifting high into the air from the peak of the cone. He had heard Grandfather Ruau tell of the Smoking Islands, the home of savage tribes. They were the dark islands of the eaters-of-men. Was that distant island one such? Perhaps this very island upon which he stood belonged to them, too! It was a terrible thought.

As he stood there surveying his world, the wind that

swept up from the wide Pacific beat hard against him, whistling in his ears. Almost he had to lean against it to keep his balance. It was a southwest wind that blew straight from the Smoking Island, whipping the sea to anger. Inside the barrier-reef the water deepened and shoaled in changing hues. Up here the whole world seemed consumed with light and color. Far off a mist of gulls drifted above the breaking surf, their hoarse cries as unceasing as the hum within a shell. Towering above Mafatu's head, the basalt cone of the island looked as soft in hue as an amethyst, broken and worn by a thousand years of wind and storm.

He observed that the barrier-reef encircled the entire island. There were only two openings in the reef through which canoes might enter. One opening lay on the side of the island where Mafatu had been cast ashore; the other was here to the southwest, facing the distant Smoking Island. In each case the opening was caused by a river which flowed from the mountain down into the lagoon; for the tiny coral polyp which builds up its ramparts from the floor of the sea cannot withstand fresh water. Wherever a river flows into the sea there will be a breach in the barrier-reef.

Mafatu jumped in alarm as a wild boar crashed through the undergrowth. It was so close that the boy caught a glimpse of its dark hide. Uri leaped in pursuit, barking furiously. Mafatu relaxed, and a smile crossed his face. Pig roasted underground in the hot oven stones of the *umu*— *Aué!* His mouth watered at the golden prospect. He would make a spear and kill the *puaa*, that's what he would do! He was fired with excitement and set for the adventure. Then the thought of killing a wild boar in single-handed combat struck him dumb with wonder. Why, he would never have dreamed of such a thing in Hikueru! He was Mafatu, the Boy Who Was Afraid. . . . He set his jaw with fierce resolution. He had never known a man who killed a wild pig. But Grandfather Ruau, who had traveled as far as distant Tahiti, had told how the warriors of that island killed pigs in the mountains with naught but a knife for a weapon, bracing themselves so that the animal impaled itself upon the blade. It needed a strong arm, and a stouter heart. Could he, Mafatu, ever accomplish such a feat? Grandfather brought back with him a necklace made from the curling tusks of the boar, and Mafatu could remember to this day how the dark-blue scrolls of tattooing on the old man's copper flesh set off the handsome ivory teeth. That necklace was the envy of every man in Hikueru and its possession earned Grandfather much respect.

"I will make such a necklace for myself from the tusks," the boy promised bravely. "And when I return to Hikueru men will look up to me and say: 'There goes Mafatu. He killed the wild boar single-handed!' And Tavana Nui, my father, will be filled with pride."

The prospect of returning home set another train of thought in motion. "I must find a tree, a tamanu, for my canoe," the boy said aloud. "I will burn it out, then make

an adze of basalt to finish it. I'll plait a sail of pandanus. And oh, it will be a wonderful canoe!"

At that moment his eye fell upon a mango tree loaded with juicy fruit, and he plucked a fruit and sank his teeth into the rosy pulp. For a few seconds while he ate his fill and the juices ran down over his chin, he forgot all about his canoe; forgot that he needed shelter, food, fire, and weapons. Then, his hunger satisfied, his mind ran ahead again to the happy day when he would set sail for Hikueru, with all his demons put to rout and the bright flame of courage burning in his heart. Never again would he be called Mafatu, the Boy Who Was Afraid. He stood there taut with purpose, high above the demon sea.

"Maui, God of the Fishermen, hear me!" he pleaded. "I shall return home one day, I swear it. My father, Tavana Nui, will be filled with pride at my homecoming. It is a vow that I take now, O Maui. I have spoken." . . .

The wind from the sea swept up around him, its voice warm and soft and reassuring in his ear. Maui, God of the Fishermen, had heard and answered.

Mafatu decided that before he retraced his steps to his own beach he would explore the opposite side of the island. The trail dropped from the plateau in a series of swift turns and spirals. The boy clambered down, slipping and sliding, catching hold of roots and vines to keep from falling. Far below, a cool dark stream wound its way through a sheltered valley. Perhaps in that valley he would find some people.

At the base of the ancient crater, long ridges of lava descended to the valley. Of a sudden Mafatu remembered an old tale out of his childhood: he had been told how the youths of Tahiti slid down the lava slide on sleds of giant leaves! The thought had scarcely struck him before he was wrenching off half a dozen great leaves from a near-by banana tree. Even as he did so he stopped, suddenly alert. They were splendid trees, three times his own height, with broad leaves that waved in the wind like tattered banners. But what caught and held his attention were the stems where fruit had grown: they had been severed cleanly by a knife! His heart gave a great thump and hung fire.

He examined the stems with care. Tree after tree had been stripped of fruit, and within a week, too. Who had cut these bananas? Well—he would have to find out! His lips were grim as he set about making his "sled." He bound the leaves together with a fibrous rope of vines and soon had a toboggan as long as his body. When Mafatu reached the lava slide, he set his sled in place and flung himself down upon it. With a shout and a shove he was off.

Down the natural slide he sped at terrifying speed. Trees whizzed past. Wind drove the air from his nostrils. The valley rushed to meet him. He brought up with a bump in a thicket of *cassi*. As he extricated himself from the thorns he was still breathing with excitement. *Aué*, but that was fun! He did not stop to think how he would regain his plateau, for at that moment his eye fell upon a broad, well-defined path leading down through the jungle.

45

"*Aiá!*" he exclaimed. "This fine trail was never made by the feet of wild pigs!"

The boy stood there irresolute and uncertain. Some premonition of danger kept him poised, alert, and wary. He was half tempted to retrace his way and explore no further. Then an overpowering desire to know who had made that path urged him onward. The trail led toward the sea, widening as it went. Soon it opened into a cleared circle some hundred feet in circumference. Involuntarily Mafatu started forward, then drew back with a sharp cry. What he beheld filled him with awe and it set him trembling.

He saw a series of wide stone terraces rising in a pyramid many feet high; on top of this pyramid a grotesque idol, hideously ugly, reared in the brilliant sunshine. It was an ancient idol, its contours softened with fungus and lichens, corroded by the rains of ages. The roots of convolvulus writhed about its base. No wind reached this hidden circle, and insects hummed in the hot air. Mafatu felt that he was stifling. His heart pounded. A *marae*—a Sacred Place. . . .

Scarcely daring to breathe, he advanced a step. Then he drew up short. Around the base of the idol he saw piles of bones, charred, but not old. The platform was strewn with them. Bones too large for dogs, too large for pigs. And then Mafatu understood. His heart congealed. This was a *motu tabu*, a Forbidden Island. Here the eaters-of-men made their terrible sacrifices to the *Varua Ino*.

46

Mafatu stood rooted, unable to advance, powerless to flee. Uri slunk at his side growling low, the hair on his neck lifting stiffly. Involuntarily the boy looked up; through an opening in the trees the cloud-cone of Smoking Island floated on a wine-colored sea. . . . Could that distant island be the home of the savages who used this *motu tabu* for their Place of Sacrifice? Was it here that they came in their black canoes to turn the night hideous with their drums and ceremonies and leaping fires? Mafatu shivered. He had believed that Maui, God of the Fishermen, had led him safe to this island. But perhaps after all it had been only a cruel prank of Moana, the Sea God, angry at having been cheated. The boy seemed to hear Moana saying: "Someday, someday, Mafatu, I will claim you." . . .

It was evident that the savages had been here recently, for the piles of ashes rested undisturbed by wind and storm. The cleared circle seemed to hold its breath, locked in a supernatural silence.

As the boy paused, irresolute, looking up at the towering marae, his eye was caught and held by a gleam of light and his heart gave a mighty leap. For he saw that a spearhead lay on the sacred platform. Finely ground, sharp-edged; a spear for food, a weapon against attack. Dare he take it? It might mean death. . . . His heart pounded. He moved one foot forward. His hands were damp and cold. The flashing spearhead winked back at him like an evil eye. The boy's limbs turned to water. For a second he was powerless to move. In that moment had a score of black men leaped

48

forth from the jungle he could not have stirred or cried. He fought himself for control. Taking a deep breath, he whispered: "It is you, Maui, who have led me to this island. I know it. Do not forsake me now!"

Almost it seemed as if he could see dark shadows moving among the ferns and hear the phantom whisper of voices. But he edged forward, poised for instant flight. There—he was so close to the idol that he could have touched it. He reached out his hand. It took every ounce of will. The spearhead glistened brightly. . . . His fingers closed about it, tightened. The towering idol cast a shadow of darkness across the green earth. Quickly the boy drew the spearhead toward him. But in moving it he dislodged a bone. It fell at his feet. Its touch was deathly cold. Mafatu gasped. Then he whipped about and was running, running. But he still gripped the spearhead in his fist.

He scrambled back up the path whence he had come. His heart was hammering, his leg stiff and sore. The twisted roots of the *mapé* trees reached for him as he fled. Never had they seemed so much like grasping fingers. The giant tree-ferns turned the jungle to an eerie gloom. The boy was filled with unaccountable dread. His limbs seemed weighted. When at last he reached the base of the lava slide, he turned at right angles and fought his way upward, hauling, pulling himself by vines.

At last he gained the plateau—drew up breathless and panting. The spear flashed in his hand. He looked down at it in wonder. Nothing had happened to him! He had touched the marae, dislodged a bone on the place *tabu*, yet still he lived. The sun shone. The sky arched blue. Nothing was changed. And this spear, *aué!* But it was a beautiful one! It was worth all the risk. Those eaters-of-men had wrought well. Now he, Mafatu, could kill the wild pig! Now he could defend himself against attack.

But, most important of all, he knew that he had won a great victory over himself. He had forced himself to do something that he dreaded, something that took every ounce of his will. The taste of victory salted his lips. He threw out his chest and cried: "It is you, Maui, who have helped me! My thanks, my thanks to you!" Uri leaped and pranced with excitement at his master's side.

Back once more at his own shelter, Mafatu kept looking and looking at the spear. Happiness flooded through him in warm tides. It was not so much the possession of a spear. No . . . it was the fact that he had touched the marae. That took courage, *ai*, courage! And as he set about searching for a firestick he sang a song at the top of his young lungs. It was a brave song of Taaroa, the hero-god who rose out of the sea to slay the enemies of his people:

> "Taaroa puai e!
> Hiti raa no te moana,
> Horoa te puai ia'u,
> Taaroa e!"

His voice rose clear and strong across the jungle stillness. Sea birds and parakeets hushed their cries to listen to the strange, intruding sound.

At last Mafatu found a firestick to his liking: a piece of hard wood, bone-dry, as large around as his forearm. Then he searched for a smaller piece of the same wood. Propping the larger piece against a rock, he squatted on his haunches before it and gripped the small sliver in both hands. He began to move it back and forth, back and forth upon the hard surface. A groove commenced to form. A little pile of wood dust gathered at one extremity of the groove. Now the boy's hands were moving faster and faster. Back and forth they flew, while perspiration stood out on his forehead and his breath came in gasps. At last he was rewarded. A wisp of smoke drifted upward from the wood dust. A glow. . . . The boy seized a few twigs and, cupping his hands with great care, blew upon the spark. A flame burst into life.

He had made fire.

Weary with the exertion, Mafatu settled back on his haunches and watched the leaping flame. *Fire!* His arms and back ached unmercifully; the wound in his leg throbbed. But the warm glow of flame comforted him. It made him think of home, of food and warmth and companionship; of faces around the evening circle; of the drone of old men's voices, telling their endless tales of daring. And he was swept by a sudden wave of loneliness, a longing for the sound of his father's deep voice. . . . He shut his lips tight and fought it back, then leaped to his feet and set about his small tasks with a great show of business. He would not think of those things. He would not remember—if he could help it. Now he would have cooked food, warmth when he was wet through, and the first implement with which to set about building his canoe. Tomorrow he would fell a tree by fire and start to work upon his dugout. He would make fire only by day, and then not too large a blaze, for its glow might be visible on the distant island of the eaters-of-men. Thus he forced his thoughts into safer channels.

He threw breadfruit into the fire. There it would stay until it was charred black and thoroughly cooked. Next, he laid half a dozen *fei*—wild bananas—in the coals, covering them with wet leaves so that slowly they would steam through. While his dinner was cooking, he had yet another task to do. He set about it at once: he tore off half a dozen fronds of a low-growing coconut tree; then he began to plait them into flat, matlike screens. These, made into a lean-to, would be his shelter against wind and storm. Several layers of them would be water-tight.

"If only I had my knife, Uri," the boy groaned. "How simple it would be! I must search the lagoon for a *pahua* shell. It grinds down to a fine cutting edge. We'll soon have a good knife."

Uri thought so, too; that was evident from the motion of his tireless tail.

"Perhaps," Mafatu thought suddenly, "I might find a knife at the Sacred Place of the eaters-of-men." Then he shook his head. "No! I shall never return to that terrible marae *tabu!*"

But each day, he resolved, he would climb to the high plateau, his lookout to the southwest. Someday, someday the eaters-of-men would come back. Before long, perhaps. . . . Mafatu was certain of it, as he was certain that the sun shone and was warm. It was inevitable. And when the black men came, he would have to leave, or die.

The boy looked fondly at the tamanu tree that he had marked already for his canoe. "Tomorrow I shall start work upon it," he promised. "And *aiá*, what a canoe I shall build! Deep and strong, but light. An outrigger as swift and powerful as a shark's tail. And when my father sees it he will say: '*Aué*, my son, but they build fine canoes in that island you have come from.' And then I will say: 'But I built it myself, my father.' And then he will say: '*Aiá!* Is it possible—this fine canoe?' "

The fire blazed brightly and the breadfruit gave forth a tempting odor. Jets of vapor rose from the steaming bananas. Uri snuggled down at his master's side and Mafatu hugged the dog close. "*Ai*, there's food for you, too, my brother," he cried. "And tomorrow we shall have fish. See my spear, how bravely it flashes! I will make a new shaft for it, and then I shall kill the *ma'o*, the shark! And the wild pig, too. *Ai*, Uri, you will see!"

The boy pulled the breadfruit from the fire and broke it in half. Its white, flaky meat was packed with sustenance; a little like bread in taste, a trifle like potato, better than either. The boy gave half of it to Uri. The dog circled around, sniffing longingly as he waited for his dinner to cool. The bananas popped from their skins while their juices bubbled in the heat. Deftly Mafatu slid them out of the fire, transferred them to a broad leaf that served as a plate. Then, unmindful of burned fingers, he fell upon the hot food. He was famished. It seemed that he had never been so hungry in his whole life, and for a time there was only the sound of his greedy munching. Never had food tasted so good!

He ate and ate, until his stomach could hold no more. Then a great weariness stole through his limbs. With a sigh of deep content he sank back upon the cool sand and closed his eyes. Uri snuggled close, warm and friendly against his side. Overhead, the plaited fronds of the palms formed a snug shelter. "Someday," the boy thought drowsily, "I will make my roof water-tight, but not yet." . . .

The tide was running out of the lagoon with the sunset in a whispering hum of sound, like the reassuring hush of a mother to her child. Mafatu lay there under his lean-to, relaxed in every nerve. He had fire, food, shelter. He had faced Moana, the Sea God. He had dared the sacred marae of the eaters-of-men to win his spear. There was a new-found confidence singing in his heart. He had found a new belief in himself.

At peace with himself and his world, he slept.

4. DRUMS

THE very next morning Mafatu set about building his canoe. He had banked his fire the night before in the natural shelter of a cave and he resolved never to let the sparks die out. For it was altogether too difficult to make fire with the firestick, and it required too much time. In Hikueru, for that reason, the fires were always kept burning, and it was the special charge of the younger members of a family to see that fuel was ever at hand. Woe unto the small boy who let the family fires go out!

While his breakfast roasted in the coals, the boy cleared the brush away from the base of the great tamanu. There was no wood better for canoe building than this. It was tough, durable, yet buoyant in the water. Mafatu could fell his tree by fire, and burn it out, too. Later he would grind an adze out of basalt for the finished work. The adze would take a long time, but he had made them often in Hikueru and he knew just how to go about it. The boy was beginning to realize that the hours he had spent fashioning utensils were to stand him now in good stead. Nets and knives and sharkline, implements and shell fishhooks—he knew how to make them all. How he had hated those tasks in Hikueru! He was quick and clever with his hands, and now he was grateful for the skill which was his.

The fire crackled and snapped about the base of the tamanu tree. When at length it had eaten well into the trunk, Mafatu climbed aloft and crept cautiously out upon a large branch that overhung the beach. Then taking firm hold of the branches above his head, he began to jump up and down. As the fire ate deeper into the trunk, the tree began to lean under the boy's weight. With a snap and a crash it fell across the sand. As it fell, Mafatu leaped free of the branches, as nimbly as a cat.

"That's enough for today, Uri," he decided. "Tomorrow we'll build our fires down the trunk and start burning it out. When the eaters-of-men come, we will be ready!"

In the meantime there were many other things to do: a

fish trap of bamboo, a net of sennit, a fishhook, too, if only he could find some bone. And while the canoe was building, how could Mafatu get out to the distant reef to set his trap, unless first he made a raft of bamboo?

The boy decided that the raft was of first importance. He chose a score or more of fine bamboos as large around as his arm, felling them by fire; then he lashed them together with strips of *purau* bark, making a sturdy raft of two thicknesses. It would serve him well until his canoe should be finished.

As he worked, his mind returned again and again to the wild pig he was determined to kill. How could he go back to Hikueru without a boar's-tooth necklace? Why, that necklace was almost as important as a canoe! For by that token men would know his strength and courage. When the day came that he should leave this high island, he would sail to the north and east. Somewhere in that quarter lay the Cloud of Islands; the great Tuamotu Archipelago which extends across a thousand miles of ocean and ten degrees of latitude. Within those reef-spiked channels floated Hikueru, his homeland. . . . There was no doubt in his mind that he would find it; for Maui, who had led him safe to this shore, would someday guide him home again. But first, Mafatu knew, he must prove himself worthy. Men should never again call him Mafatu, the Boy Who Was Afraid. And Tavana Nui should say with pride: "Here is my son, come home from the sea."

Kivi, the albatross, came and went on his mysterious errands, emerging out of blue space, vanishing into it again. At sundown, regularly, the white bird came wheeling and circling, to alight clumsily on the beach almost at Mafatu's side, while Uri pranced about and greeted his friend after his own fashion. As for Uri, he was having the time of his life; for there were countless sea birds nesting along the shore to be chased and put to rout; and wild goats and pigs in the mountains to make life exciting enough for any dog.

Mafatu had discovered a mulberry tree. He stripped off the bark and removed the inner white lining. Then he wet the fiber and laid it upon a flat stone and set about beating it with a stick of wood. The fiber spread and grew thinner under the persistent beating. The boy added another strip, wet it, and beat it into the first one; then another and another. Soon he had a yard of "cloth" to serve as a *pareu*. It was soft and white, and now at last he was clothed.

"Before I go home I will make a dye of *ava* and paint a fine design on my *pareu*," the boy promised himself. "I must not go back ill-clothed and empty-handed. Men must know that I have conquered the sea, and made the land serve me as well."

The days passed in a multitude of tasks that kept Mafatu busy from dawn till dark. His lean-to grew into a three-sided house with bamboo walls and a thatch of palm leaves. The fourth wall was open to the breezes of the lagoon. It was a trim little house and he was proud of it. A roll of woven mats lay on the floor; there was a shelf in the wall with three bowls cut from coconut shells; bone fish-hooks dangled from a peg; there was a coil of tough sennit, many feet long; an extra *pareu* of tapa waterproofed with gum of the *artu* tree, for wet weather. All day long the wind played through the openings in the bamboo walls and at night lizards scurried through the thatch with soft rustlings.

One morning, wandering far down the beach, Mafatu came upon a sheltered cove. His heart gave a leap of joy; for there, white-gleaming in the sun, was all that remained of the skeleton of a whale. It might not have meant very much to you or to me; but to Mafatu it meant knives and fishhooks galore, splintered bone for darts and spears, a shoulder blade for an ax. It was a veritable treasure trove. The boy leaped up and down in his excitement. "Uri!" he shouted. "We're rich! Come—help me drag these bones home!"

His hands seemed all thumbs in his eagerness; he tied as many bones as he could manage into two bundles. One bundle he shouldered himself. The other Uri dragged behind him. And thus they returned to the camp site, weary, but filled with elation. Even the dog seemed to have some understanding of what this discovery meant; or if not, he was at least infected with his master's high spirits. He leaped about like a sportive puppy, yapping until he was hoarse.

Now began the long process of grinding the knife and the ax. Hour after long hour, squatting before a slab of basalt, Mafatu worked and worked, until his hands were raw and blistered and the sweat ran down into his eyes. The knife emerged first, since that was the most imperative. Its blade was ten inches long, its handle a knob of joint. It was sharp enough to cut the fronds of coconut trees, to slice off the end of a green nut. *Ai*, but it was a splendid knife! All Mafatu's skill went into it. It would be a fine weapon as well, the boy thought grimly, as he ground it down to a sharp point. Some sea robber had been breaking into his bamboo trap and he was going to find out who the culprit was! Probably that old hammerhead shark who was always cruising around. . . . Just as if he owned the lagoon!

Fishing with a line took too long when you were working against time. Mafatu could not afford to have his trap robbed. Twice it had been broken into, the stout bamboos crushed and the contents eaten. It was the work either of a shark or of an octopus. That was certain. No other fish was strong enough to snap the tough bamboo.

Mafatu's mouth was set in a grim line as he worked away on his knife. That old hammerhead—undoubtedly *he* was the thief! Mafatu had come to recognize him; for every day when the boy went out with his trap, that shark, larger than all the others, was circling around, wary and watchful. The other sharks seemed to treat the hammerhead with deference.

Hunger alone drove Mafatu out to the reef to set his trap. He knew that if he was to maintain strength to accomplish all that lay ahead he must have fish to add to his diet of fruit. But often as he set his trap far out by the barrier-reef, the hammerhead would approach, roll over slightly in passing, and the cold gleam of its eye filled Mafatu with dread and anger.

"Wait, you!" the boy threatened darkly, shaking his fist at the *ma'o*. "Wait until I have my knife! You will not be so brave then, Ma'o. You will run away when you see it flash."

But the morning that the knife was finished, Mafatu did not feel so brave as he would have liked. He hoped he would never see the hammerhead again. Paddling out to the distant reef, he glanced down from time to time at the long-bladed knife where it hung about his neck by a cord of sennit. It wasn't, after all, such a formidable weapon. It was only a knife made by a boy from a whale's rib.

Uri sat on the edge of the raft, sniffing at the wind. Mafatu always took his dog along, for Uri howled unmercifully if he were left behind. And Mafatu had come to rely upon the companionship of the little yellow dog. The boy talked with the animal as if he were another person, consulting with him, arguing, playing when there was time for play. They were very close, these two.

This morning as they approached the spot where the fish trap was anchored, Mafatu saw the polished dorsal of the hated hammerhead circling slowly in the water. It was like a triangle of black basalt, making a little furrow in the water as it passed.

"*Aiá*, Ma'o!" the boy shouted roughly, trying to bolster up his courage. "I have my knife today, see! Coward who robs traps—catch your own fish!"

The hammerhead approached the raft in leisurely fashion; it rolled over slightly, and its gaping jaws seemed to curve in a yawning grin. Uri ran to the edge of the raft, barking furiously; the hair on the dog's neck stood up in a bristling ridge. The shark, unconcerned, moved away. Then with a whip of its powerful tail it rushed at the bamboo fish trap and seized it in its jaws. Mafatu was struck dumb. The hammerhead shook the trap as a terrier might shake a rat. The boy watched, fascinated, unable to make a move. He saw the muscles work in the fish's neck as the great tail thrashed the water to fury. The trap splintered into bits, while the fish within escaped only to vanish into the shark's mouth. Mafatu was filled with impotent rage. The hours he had spent making that trap— But all he could do was shout threats at his enemy.

Uri was running from one side of the raft to the other, furious with excitement. A large wave sheeted across the reef. At that second the dog's shift in weight tipped the raft at a perilous angle. With a helpless yelp, Uri slid off into the water. Mafatu sprang to catch him but he was too late.

Instantly the hammerhead whipped about. The wave slewed the raft away. Uri, swimming frantically, tried to

regain it. There was desperation in the brown eyes—the puzzled eyes so faithful and true. Mafatu strained forward. His dog. His companion. . . . The hammerhead was moving in slowly. A mighty rage stormed through the boy. He gripped his knife. Then he was over the side in a clean-curving dive.

Mafatu came up under his enemy. The shark spun about. Its rough hide scraped the flesh from the boy's shoulder. In that instant Mafatu stabbed. Deep, deep into the white belly. There was a terrific impact. Water lashed to foam. Stunned, gasping, the boy fought for life and air.

It seemed that he would never reach the surface. *Aué*, his lungs would burst! . . . At last his head broke water. Putting his face to the surface, he saw the great shark turn over, fathoms deep. Blood flowed from the wound in its belly. Instantly gray shapes rushed in—other sharks, tearing the wounded hammerhead to pieces.

Uri—where was he? Mafatu saw his dog then. Uri was trying to pull himself up on the raft. Mafatu seized him by the scruff and dragged him up to safety. Then he caught his dog to him and hugged him close, talking to him foolishly. Uri yelped for joy and licked his master's cheek.

It wasn't until Mafatu reached shore that he realized what he had done. He had killed the *ma'o* with his own hand, with naught but a bone knife. He could never have done it for himself. Fear would have robbed his arm of all strength. He had done it for Uri, his dog. And he felt suddenly humble, with gratitude.

Now the adze was completed. Thus the canoe, too, was beginning to take finished shape. It was fifteen feet long, three feet deep, and scarcely a foot wide. Often as he worked, the boy would pause to stand off and admire his craft. It was a beautiful canoe! How proud his father would be. . . . Alas that it was such slow work.

When the hull had been hollowed out, it must be smoothed off with the adze and caulked with *artu* gum. Then a mast must be made of pukatea, straight and true; a sail woven from pandanus. And there was rigging to be made of sennit, tough and strong as wire. The craft would have been finished sooner if only there were not so many things to interfere. Every day, for example, Mafatu climbed the plateau to his lookout. He had not missed one day since he arrived at the island. He knew that when the eaters-of-men came they would sail by day; they would have to beat against the prevailing wind. It would take them many hours to come from Smoking Island. Mafatu would be able to see them from his lookout long before they arrived. If only he could be ready before they came! He must, he must! But that trip up the mountain every day took so much precious time. His canoe would have been finished days ago, but for that.

"Today I will not go," the boy thought, as his adze whirred and chipped. "It takes too long."

Then he sighed and laid down the adze. Caution was the better part of wisdom. He picked up his shining spear with its new shaft and turned toward the trail that led to the high plateau. Uri leaped ahead, his nose keen-pointed to the ground.

This day as Mafatu climbed the rough trail through the jungle, he was preoccupied, lost in his thoughts. His mind was not in this business at all: he was thinking about the rigging of his canoe, planning how he could strengthen it here, tighten it there. Some instinct of danger must have made him pause, warning him to beware. There it was— just a rustle in the undergrowth. Scarcely louder than an insect's hum. The boy drew up tense and listening. Uri had dashed off on some wild-goose chase of his own. The boy stood rooted, alert. He saw it then: a wild boar with lowered head. Eyes red with hate. The flash of its wicked tusks.

The animal pawed the ground suddenly. Its grunting snort broke the stillness. Mafatu knew a blind impulse to turn and run. Then he drew a deep breath and shouted out a challenge:

"*Puaa viri!* Wild pig! I, Mafatu, have come to kill you!"

The boar charged. Over the ground it tore. Foam flew back from its tusks. The boy braced himself. He met the charge with a perfectly timed thrust of the spear. The boar impaled itself, shoulder-deep, upon the spearhead.

Mafatu was thrown off balance, sent spinning headlong. Over and over he rolled. He leaped to his feet in a panic, defenseless. But the boar toppled, gave a convulsive shudder, lay still.

Mafatu was struck dumb. He had killed a wild pig! For a second he could not grasp the wonderful truth of it. Then he leaped wildly into the air, shouting: "*Aué te aué!* I have killed the *puaa!* Do you hear me, Tavana Nui? I, your son, have killed a boar! Ho! Ha!"

Uri came leaping out of the jungle and barked himself hoarse at sight of the pig.

"A fine one you are!" Mafatu joked at his dog. "Where were you when I needed you? Off chasing butterflies, that's you! Was it for this I saved you from the teeth of the *ma'o?* I've a mind not to give you one mouthful of *puaa.*"

Uri hung his head and dropped his tail, then brightened as Mafatu laughed joyously. "Foolish one! Here—drag your share."

The boy made a rude sled of bamboo and loaded the heavy animal onto it. Then he hitched a stout liana about Uri's neck and the dog threw his weight into the task. The two started home in triumph with their burden, Mafatu singing at the top of his lungs a lusty song of blood and battle. He was all Polynesian now, charged with the ancient fierceness of his race. Victory coursed like fire through his veins. There was nothing he would not have dared! Nothing he feared! *Aiá,* but life was good!

When they reached the camp site, Mafatu built up a roaring fire and set a pile of stones to heat. While the stones were heating, the boy cleaned the pig at the water's edge, then stuffed its empty belly with succulent *ti* leaves and red bananas. When at last the oven stones were white and smoking, Mafatu dragged the pig back to the fire and rolled it upon the hot *umu.* Then he covered it with layer upon layer of plantain leaves—dozens of them—to hold in the steam and to allow the pork to cook through slowly. Uri leaped about, sniffing at the delicious odors, barking his delight. *Pork!* After weeks of fish and fish and fish, how good it would taste! Besides, fish was not good for dogs. Too many bones. Kivi, no meat eater, looked on calmly, wondering what all this disturbance was about; the bird was content with a coconut that Mafatu split open for him, that he might join in the feast.

Mafatu's mouth fairly watered in anticipation. But even as he settled back to await the feast, his hands were busy: the sun gleamed brightly on the curving tusks that already he was making into a necklace. They formed almost a complete circle and were as white as bleached coral. *Aué!* How men's tongues would chatter when they saw this fine necklace! Even Grandfather's had been no finer.

A strange picture on that lonely beach under the palms: a pig roasting on a fire; a boy lean and brown and whip-strong, making a boar's-tooth necklace; a prancing yellow dog; a calm, wide-winged albatross pecking at a coconut.

Mafatu slipped the necklace about his throat, and he could fairly feel its magic charging him with strength! He pulled the oven stones away from the *umu*, and there lay the pig, golden, glowing, done to a turn. Rich juices ran in little rivulets down its sides. And as Mafatu ate, one thought alone filled his mind, overshadowing even his enjoyment of this rare feast: soon, soon now he would be ready. He had killed the *ma'o*. The *puaa*, too. His canoe

would soon be completed. And then—then he would return to Hikueru!

The canoe was finished.

Mafatu lashed the tough *purau* outrigger into place with hands that trembled. The woven sail was complete and ready; the rigging strong as wire. There—it was all over! The boy could hardly wait to get his craft into water.

Placing logs under the curving stem, he gave a shove and a push. The canoe stirred, moved forward, quick with life. Another shove and the craft slid into the lagoon. And there it floated lightly, easily as a gull poised for flight. Mafatu stood back and surveyed it with shining eyes. He could hardly believe that all these weeks of labor were at an end. Suddenly he was quiet. With lifted head he offered up the prayer with which all ships were launched at Hikueru:

> "Taaroa, Mighty One!
> My thanks to you
> In this task completed.
> Guide it on your back
> To safe harbor.
> Taaroa, *e!*"

The boy leaped into the stern, picked up the paddle, and ran up the sail. Uri sprang into the bow, yelping for very joy. Kivi sailed far overhead on widespread wings. The breeze caught the sail, swelled it to a golden curve. The outrigger leaned at a sharp angle and sped ahead toward the distant reef. Spray flew back from the prow and Mafatu's heart beat high. He let out the sheet, wrapped the sennit rope around his foot, and gripped the steering paddle with both hands. He was filled with pride in his canoe. Never had he been as happy as in this moment.

Out toward the black reef, closer and closer the canoe skimmed on a wide arc of speed. It was late afternoon and the sun was setting in a blaze of glory, but the boy was reluctant to turn back. He knew that he should have climbed to the lookout that morning. This was the first day he had neglected that duty. But the temptation to complete his canoe had been too great. Tomorrow at daybreak he would climb the plateau for the last time. And then—and then Hikueru!

As the little craft skimmed out toward the barrier-reef, the thunder of the surf increased in volume to an overwhelming sound. Waves, born far south in the Antarctic ice fields—the home of all waves—broke their backs upon this coral rampart. Gathering far out, they charged the reef: sea horses with flinging manes of foam. The surf shot skyward and above its mist sea gulls swooped and darted. The reef thunder no longer filled Mafatu with unease. He had lived too close to it these past weeks. Out here, half a mile from shore, detached from all security of the land, he had come to believe that at last he had established a truce with Moana, the Sea God. His skill against the ocean's might.

The boy skirted along the edge of the reef, lowered his

sail, and dropped overboard the lump of coral which served as anchor. Then he took out his fishline and baited the hook with a piece of crab meat. He wanted to enjoy to the full this new sensation of confidence in himself, this freedom from the sea's threat. He looked back at the land fondly, but without longing. The high peak, purple in the waning light, stood somber against the sky. The valleys were shadowed with mystery. All these weeks he had lived close to this island and been grateful for its bounty. But he had been born on an atoll—a low island—and all his life had been spent in the spaciousness of open sea and wind-swept palms. There was something gloomy and oppressive in this high island. The reef—this was a part of his heritage. The sea, at last, was as much his element as the land.

The realization flooded through him in a warm tide of content. He lowered his fishline, fastened it to the mid-thwart, and looked deep down into the clear water. He saw a scarlet rock-cod materialize, hang in the shadow of the canoe, motionless save for the slight movement of its gills. With a sudden flip of the tail it vanished.

How fantastic was that undersea world! The boy saw branching staghorn corals, as large as trees, through which jellyfishes floated like a film of fog. He saw shoals of tiny mullet, miniature arrowheads—the whole school scarcely larger than a child's hand. A conger eel drew its ugly head back within a shadowy cavern.

Here beside the wall of reef Mafatu's bamboo fish trap hung suspended; before he returned to shore he would empty the trap. It had been undisturbed since the hammer-head was killed, and each day had yielded up a good supply of mullet or crayfish or lobsters. Here the wall of living coral descended to the lagoon floor. Its sides were pierced with caves of darkness whose mystery the boy felt no desire to explore. Far below, perhaps forty feet, the sandy floor of the lagoon was clear and green in the dappled light. A parrot fish emerged from the gloom, nibbled at Mafatu's bait, then vanished.

"*Aué!* These fish must be well fed. My piece of crab meat does not tempt them."

The boy decided to give it up and content himself with the fish in the bamboo trap. He leaned over the gunwale

73

and pulled it up out of water. Through the openings in the cage he could see three lobsters, blue-green and fat. What luck! But as he dragged the heavy, wet trap over the gunwale, the fiber cord that fastened his knife about his neck caught on an end of bamboo. The trap slipped. The cord snapped. The knife fell into the water.

With dismay the boy watched it descend. It spiraled rapidly, catching the sunlight as it dropped down, down to the sandy bottom. And there it lay, just under the edge of a branching staghorn. Mafatu eyed it uncertainly. His knife—the knife he had labored so hard to shape. . . . He knew what he ought to do: he should dive and retrieve it. To make another knife so fine would take days. Without it he was seriously handicapped. He *must* get his knife! But . . .

The reef-wall looked dark and forbidding in the fading light. Its black holes were the home of the giant *feké*—the octopus. . . . The boy drew back in sudden panic. He had never dived as deep as this. It might be even deeper than he thought, for the clarity of the water confused all scale of distance. The knife looked so very near, and yet . . . There it lay, gleaming palely.

The boy gazed down at it with longing. He remembered the morning he had found the whale's skeleton; the first one he had ever seen. Surely Maui, God of the Fishermen, had sent the whale there to die for Mafatu's use! The long hours that had gone into the making of the knife. . . . It had saved Uri's life, too. And now Uri, in the bow of the

74

canoe, was looking at his master with eyes so puzzled and true.

Mafatu drew a deep breath. How could he abandon his knife? Would Maui (the thought chilled him) think him a coward? Was he still Mafatu, the Boy Who Was Afraid?

He leaped to his feet, gave a brave hitch to his *pareu*. Then he was overside in the water. He clung for a moment to the gunwale, breathing deeply. Inhaling, then releasing the air in a long-drawn whistle, he prepared his lungs for the pressure of the depths. Many times he had seen the pearl divers do it. In the canoe lay a coral weight fastened to a length of sennit. Mafatu took this weight and held the cord in his toes. With a final deep breath he descended feet-first, allowing the weight to pull him downward. At about twenty feet he released the weight, turned over, and swam for the bottom.

Here the water was cool and green. The sunlight filtered from above in long, oblique bands. Painted fishes fled before him. He saw a giant *pahua*, a clam shell, five feet across and taller than he: its open lips waiting to snap shut upon fish or man. Green fronds waved gently as if in some submarine wind. A shadow moved above the boy's head and he glanced upward in alarm: only a sand shark cruising harmlessly. . . . An eel, like a cold waving ribbon, touched his leg and was gone.

The knife—there it lay. How sharp and bright it looked. Now the boy's hands were upon it. He seized it and sprang upward toward the light.

In that second a whiplash shot out from a cavern at his back: a lash like a length of rubber hose. The boy caught the flash of vacuum cups that lined its under surface. Panic stabbed him. The *feké*—the octopus! Another lash whipped forth and encircled his waist. It drew taut. Then the octopus came forth from its den to face and kill its prey.

Mafatu saw a purplish globe of body, eyes baleful and fixed as fate; a parrot-mouth, cruel and beaked, that worked and wabbled. . . . Another whiplash encircled the boy's leg. The knife— Desperately Mafatu stabbed for one of the eyes. Then darkness clouded the water as the octopus siphoned out his venom. There in submarine gloom a boy fought for his life with the most dreaded monster of the deep. He could feel the sucking pressure of those terrible tentacles. . . . His wind was almost gone.

Blindly Mafatu stabbed again, this time for the other eye. The blow, so wildly driven, went true. The terrible grip relaxed, slacked. The tentacles grew limp. Then Mafatu was springing upward, upward, drawn up toward light and air and life.

When he reached the canoe he had hardly enough strength to cling to the gunwale. But cling he did, his breath coming in tearing gasps. Uri, beside himself, dashed from one end of the canoe to the other, crying piteously. Slowly strength returned to the boy's limbs, warmth to his chilled soul. He dragged himself into the canoe and collapsed on the floor. He lay there, as in a trance, for what seemed an eternity.

The sun had set. Dusk was rising from the surface of the sea. Mafatu struggled upright and peered cautiously over the side of the canoe. The inky water had cleared. Down there, forty feet below, the octopus lay like a broken shadow. The white cups of its tentacles gleamed dully in the watery gloom. With sharkline and hook the boy fished up the *feké's* body. As he dragged it into the canoe one of the tentacles brushed his ankle. Its touch was clammy and of a deathly chill. Mafatu shuddered and shrank away. He had eaten squid and small octopi ever since he was born, but he knew that he could not have touched a mouthful of this monster. He raised his spear and plunged it again and again into the body of his foe, shouting aloud a savage paean of triumph. A thousand years of warrior-heritage sounded in his cry.

Once more Maui had protected him! What to do with the *feké?* The boy decided that he would cut off the tentacles; they would dry and shrink, but they would be still of prodigious size, and the people of Hikueru would say: "See, Mafatu killed the *feké* single-handed. *Aué te aué!*"

Dusk, almost in an instant, deepened into night. As Mafatu turned the nose of his canoe toward shore, the first stars were appearing, bright and close and friendly. There was the Southern Cross, pointing toward the end of the world. . . . The lagoon was a black mirror dusted with star-shine. Far below in the dark waters, illuminated fishes moved and had their being: meteors, galaxies, constellations under the sea. The boy saw a line of light, narrow as a blade, as the rare *pala* flashed away in its everlasting quest. A sand shark, phosphorescent ghost, darted after the *pala*—seized it in a swirl of luminous mist. The mist faded slowly. It was blood. Mysterious life forces were completing their cycle in those dark depths, even as on the earth and in the air above. This sea—no more to be feared than earth or air: only another element for man to conquer. And he, Mafatu, had killed the *feké. Aué te aué!*

As he dipped his paddle with a swinging rhythm, the rhythm of his thoughts swung in unison: "Tomorrow I shall start home! Tomorrow, tomorrow! *Aiá!*"

The very thought of it set him aquiver. "Tomorrow, tomorrow!" he had been here so long. . . .

He dragged the canoe up on the beach, placed the logs under the curving stem so that he might launch it easily on the morrow. He would never need to climb the high plateau to the lookout again. Let the eaters-of-men come!

As Mafatu waited for his supper to cook, he set about preparing for his homeward journey; he would start at daybreak with the ebbing tide. He would be ready. He filled bamboo containers with fresh water, sealed them with leaves that were gummed into place, water-tight and secure. Then he stored them carefully in the canoe. He prepared a *poi* of bananas and sealed it, likewise, into containers; there it would ferment and sour and become delicious to the taste. Then he picked a score or more of green drinking nuts and flung them into the canoe. And as he trotted back and forth across the beach and his supper steamed on the fire, one thought alone, like an insistent drum beat, echoed in the boy's heart: "Tomorrow I shall start home! Tomorrow, tomorrow!"

Never again need he hang his head before his people. He had fought the sea for life and won. He had sustained himself by his own wits and skill. He had faced loneliness and danger and death, if not without flinching, at least with courage. He had been, sometimes, deeply afraid, but he had faced fear and faced it down. Surely that could be called courage.

When he lay down to sleep that night there was a profound thankfulness in his heart. "Tavana Nui," he whispered, "my father—I want you to be proud of me." . . .

He fell into a heavy, dreamless sleep.

Before dawn he was awakened by a sound of measured booming, like the beating of a supernatural drum. Thump-thump THUMP! Thump-thump THUMP! It rose above the thunder of the reef, solemn and majestic, filling the night with thunder.

Instantly awake, listening with every sense, Mafatu sat upright on the mats. Far out on the reef the seas burst and shot upward like sheeted ghosts in the moonlight. There it came again: Thump-thump THUMP! Thump-thump THUMP! Steady as a pulse, beating in the heart of darkness. . . .

And then Mafatu knew. The eaters-of-men had come.

5. HOMEWARD

A CHILL sweat broke out over Mafatu's body. He crouched there listening, unable for the moment to make a single movement. The rhythmic message that boomed across the mountain brought him a message of doom. Thump-thump THUMP! Thump-thump THUMP! It shivered along his nerves, setting his hair on edge.

Warily, moving with utmost caution, Mafatu crept out of the house. The beach was softly brilliant in the light of the waning moon. Any figure moving along the sand he could have seen instantly. He stopped, every nerve strung like a wire: the beach was deserted, the jungle silent and black with mystery. The boy rose to his feet. Swift as a shadow he turned into the undergrowth where the trail led to the high plateau. The jungle had never seemed so dark, so ominous with peril. The tormented roots of the *mapé* trees clutched at him. Lianas tripped him. Tree-ferns, ghostly in the half-light, rustled about him as he passed, their muted hush seeming to say: "Not yet, Mafatu, not yet." . . .

By the time he reached the plateau he was breathless and panting. He dropped to his knees and crawled forward, an inch or two at a time. One false move might spell destruction. But he had to know, he *had* to know. . . .

Thump-thump THUMP!

The measured booming grew louder with every inch that he advanced. Now it pounded in his ears, reverberated through his body, thrummed his nerves. Somewhere below in darkness, black hands drew forth from hollowed logs a rhythm that was a summation of life, a testament of death. Uri crept close to his master's side, the hair ridging on his neck, his growl drowned in the thunder.

Now the boy could see into the cleared circle of the Sacred Place. Leaping fires lighted a scene that burned itself forever into his memory. Fires blazed against the basalt cliffs, spurts of flame that leaped and danced, showers of sparks borne off on the back of the night wind. Now a deep wild chanting rose above the booming of the drums.

From his vantage point Mafatu saw six war canoes drawn up on the beach. Mighty canoes they were, with high-curving stems and decorations of white shell that caught the firelight in savage patterns. But what held the boy's eyes in awful trance were the figures, springing and leaping about the flames: figures as black as night's own face, darting, shifting, bounding toward the sky. The eaters-of-men. . . . Firelight glistened on their oiled bodies, on flashing spears and bristling decorations. High above the drums' tattoo rose the mournful note of the conch shells, an eerie wailing, like the voices of souls lost in interstellar space.

Mafatu saw that the savages were armed with ironwood war clubs—clubs studded with sharks' teeth or barbed with the sting-ray's spike. Zigzags of paint streaked their bodies. And towering above all, the great stone idol looked down with sightless eyes, just as it had looked for untold centuries.

Mafatu, lying there on the ledge of basalt, watched the strange scene, powerless to move, and he felt Doom itself breathing chill upon his neck. He drew back from the edge of the cliff. He must flee! In that very instant he heard a crashing in the undergrowth, not twenty yards away. A guttural shout ripped the darkness. The boy flung a desperate glance over his shoulder. Four black figures were tearing toward him through the jungle; he could see them now.

He turned and ran blindly down the trail whence he had come. Slipping, sliding, stumbling, his breath all but

choking in his throat. He felt like a man drowning in ice-cold water. He felt as he had sometimes felt in dreams, fleeing on legs that were weighted. Only one thought gave him courage as he ran: his canoe, ready and waiting. His canoe. If only he could reach it, shove it into the water before the savages overtook him. Then he would be safe. . . .

He knew this trail as he knew the back of his hand. That knowledge gave him an advantage. He could hear his pursuers, slipping, stumbling through the brush, shouting threats in a language strange to his ears. But there was no mistaking the meaning of their words.

On the boy dashed, fleet as an animal. Thorns and vines clutched at him. Once he tripped and sprawled headlong. But he was up and away in an instant. Through the trees he caught a glimpse of white beach and his heart surged. Then he was speeding across the sand, Uri at his heels.

The canoe was at the lagoon's edge. The boy fell upon the thwart, shoved the craft into the water. The logs under the stem rolled easily. In that second, the black men, yelling wildly, broke from the jungle and dashed across the beach. Mafatu was not a minute too soon. He leaped aboard and ran up the sail. The savages rushed after him into the shallows. A gust of wind filled the sail. It drew smartly. Now the men were swimming. One of them, in the lead, reached to lay hold of the outrigger. His black hand clutched the *purau* pole. The canoe slacked. Mafatu could see the gleam of bared teeth. The boy lifted the paddle and cracked it down. . . . With a groan the man dropped back into the water. The canoe, freed, skimmed out toward the barrier-reef.

The savages stopped, turned back toward shore. Then they were running back to the trail that led across the island, shouting to their fellows as they ran. Mafatu knew that it was only a question of minutes until the whole pack would be aroused and in pursuit. But he had the advantage of a head start and a light craft, while their canoes would have to beat around the southern point of the island before they could catch up with him. If only the breeze held. . . . Mafatu remembered then that the canoes he had seen drawn up on the beach had not been sailing canoes. There were strong arms to propel those black canoes, to overtake him if they could.

Mafatu's canoe, so slim and light, sped like a zephyr across the lagoon. The tide was on the ebb, churning in its race through the passage into the outer ocean. The boy gripped the steering paddle and offered up a prayer. Then he was caught in the rip-tide. The outrigger dashed through the passage, a chip on a torrent. The wind of the open sea rushed to greet it. The sail filled; the outrigger heeled over. Mafatu scrambled to windward to lend his weight for ballast. He was off! Homeward, homeward. . . .

Soon, rising above the reef thunder, the boy could hear a measured sound of savage chanting. They were after him!

Looking back over his shoulder, he could see the dark shapes of the canoes rounding the southern headland.

Moonlight shone on half a hundred wet paddles as they dipped and rose to the rhythm of the chant. It was too dark to see the eaters-of-men themselves, but their wild song grew ever more savage as they advanced.

The breeze was almost dead aft. The crab-claw sail swelled smooth and taut, rigid as a block of silver against the sky. The little canoe, so artfully built, ran with swell and favoring wind, laying knots behind her. She was as fleet and gracile as the following gulls. But the eaters-of-men were strong paddlers with death in their hearts. Their *motu tabu* had been profaned by a stranger. Vengeance powered their muscles. They were tireless. On they came.

The wind dropped. Imperceptibly at first. Sensing it, Mafatu whistled desperately for Maui. "Maui *é!* Do not desert me," he prayed. "This last time—lend me your help."

Soon the black canoes were so close that the boy could see the shine of dark bodies, the glint of teeth, and flash of ornament. If the wind died, he was lost. . . . Closer, closer the canoes advanced. There were six of them, filled each with ten warriors. Some of them leaped to their feet, brandished their clubs, shouted at the boy across the water. They were a sight to quake the stoutest heart. With every second they were cutting down the distance which separated their canoes from Mafatu's.

Then the wind freshened. Just a puff, but enough. Under its impetus the little canoe skimmed ahead while the boy's heart gave an upward surge of thanks. Maui had heard his prayer and answered.

Day broke over the wide Pacific.

There were the six black canoes, paddles flashing, now gaining, now losing. The boy was employing every art and wile of sailing that he knew. As long as the wind held he was safe. He managed his little craft to perfection, drawing from it every grace of speed in flight.

He knew that with coming night the wind might drop, and then— He forced the thought from his mind. If the wind deserted him it would mean that Maui had deserted him, too. But the savages would never get him! It would be Moana, the Sea God's turn. The boy looked down into the blue depths overside and his smile was grim: "Not yet, Moana," he muttered fiercely. "You haven't won. Not yet."

But with falling night the wind still held. Darkness rose up from the sea, enveloping the world. The stars came out clear and bright. The boy searched among them for some familiar constellation to steer by. Should it be *Mata Iki*— Little Eyes? Would *Mata Iki* lead him back safe to Hikueru? And then he saw, and knew: there, blazing bravely, were the three stars of the Fishhook of Maui. Maui —his sign. Those were his stars to steer by. They would lead him home. In that moment he was aware that the chanting of his pursuers had become fainter, steadily diminishing. At first he could not believe it. He listened intently. Yes—there was no doubt about it: as the breeze freshened, the sound grew fainter each passing moment.

The boy quenched his thirst, ate a scrap of *poi*, fought against sleep as the night waxed and waned.

By daybreak the chanting had ceased altogether. There was no sign of the canoes upon the broad expanse of the sea. The sunburst marched across the swinging waters. Far off an albatross caught the light of gold on its wings. Was it Kivi? Mafatu could not tell. The wind held fresh and fair. The high island had vanished over the curve of the sea and the eaters-of-men had vanished with it. But now the great ocean current that had carried Mafatu so willingly away from Hikueru was set dead against him.

He put his little craft first on one tack, then on another. As the long hours passed, it seemed as if he were making no headway at all, even though the canoe still cut smartly through the water. There was a drift and pull that appeared to make a forward gain impossible. Was it Moana, the implacable one, trying to prevent Mafatu from returning to his homeland?

"Perhaps," the boy thought wearily, "Maui is not yet ready for me to return. Is there still a shadow of fear in my heart? Is that it?" He was tired now in every nerve and sinew, tired in the marrow of his bones, tired of struggle.

The long hours passed slowly while the sun climbed. Mafatu lashed the steering paddle and slept fitfully. Uri lay in the shadow of the sail. The sun sank in a conflagration like the death of a world. Night came and fled. Dawn rose in a burst of flame, and still Mafatu's canoe skimmed across the sea currents, now on this tack, now on that.

He was to learn in the hours to come that all days, all time, would be like that: hours of blasting heat, of shattering sunlight; nights of fitful respite and uneasy sleep. Only the sea and the sky, the sea and the sky. A bird now and then, a fish leaping from the sea, a boy in a frail canoe. That was all.

As one day dragged into another, Mafatu scanned the heavens for some hint of rain. Storm, anything would have been a welcome relief to this blasting monotony, to this limitless circle of sea. His store of *poi* vanished. The coconuts likewise. His water was being guarded, drop by drop. But there would come a moment when the last drop must be taken, and then. . . .

The season of storm was long past. The days, as they came, were cloudless and untroubled. Each day broke like a clap of thunder and night fell softly as a footfall. The sea was sparkling and benign. The sun's rays were unbroken in their violence. At night the Fishhook of Maui twinkled down like friendly eyes, luring Mafatu on; and torch-fishes darted up from the lower depths while the black waters gleamed with strange lights. Then gradually as the canoe entered some other current of the sea, the wind slackened and diminished, this wind that had blown for him so long. Now the sail began to slat and bang in the dead air. The canoe drifted on the slow, majestic tide. The ceaseless heave and surge of the sea's dark breast lulled the boy to half-sleeping rest; the murmur of the waters playing about the prow sounded like his mother's reassuring voice.

Each sun as it rose seemed hotter than that of the preceding day. Now the face of the ocean was a disk of blazing copper. Masses of seaweed, heavy with the eggs of fishes, floated on the sluggish tide, seeming to clutch at the canoe, to hold it back from its destination. Hikueru, the Cloud of Islands—did they really exist? Were they not, like the chambered nautilus, only an iridescence dreamed by the sea? Sharks were beginning to appear—as they did always about a craft becalmed. One dorsal fin, larger than the others, followed the canoe in leisurely parallel; just far enough distant so that Mafatu could not see the body that supported it. But he knew from the size of the dorsal that it must be a tiger-shark. . . . It began at length to play upon his nerves and set him jumpy. He scarcely dared now, at night, to lash his steering paddle and sleep.

The sail slatted and banged. The boy paddled through the long hours, paddled until the muscles of his arms and shoulders ached in agony and every sinew cried in protest. And at night, when darkness brought blessed release from the sun, there was always the Fishhook of Maui leading him on. But now when the boy looked up at the ancient constellation, doubt lay heavy on his heart. Hikueru— where was it? Where was it? The sea gave back no answer.

"Maui," the boy whispered, "have you deserted me? Have you looked into my heart and found me wanting?"

And suddenly, like the snapping of a string, he was overwhelmed with despair. Maui *had* deserted him. It was Moana, the Sea God's turn. The sea looked dark and cool and inviting. Little wavelets lapped and chuckled about the hull like beckoning hands. He looked overside. Deep down in those cool depths it seemed to him that he could see faces . . . his mother's, perhaps. . . . He dashed his hand across his eyes. Had the sun stricken him daft? Had he been touched by moon-madness? Then a wave of overpowering anger brought him to his knees: anger at this dark element, this sea, which would destroy him if it could. His voice was thick and hoarse, his throat bursting with rage.

"Moana, you Sea God!" he shouted violently. *"You!* You destroyed my mother. Always you have tried to destroy me. Fear of you has haunted my sleep. Fear of you turned my people against me. But now"— he choked; his hands gripped his throat to stop its hot burning— "now I no longer fear you, Sea!" His voice rose to a wild note.

He sprang to his feet, flung back his head, spread wide his arms in defiance. "Do you hear me, Moana? I am not afraid of you! Destroy me—but I laugh at you. Do you hear? *I laugh!*"

His voice, cracked but triumphant, shattered the dead air. He sank back on his haunches, shaking with spasms of ragged laughter. It racked his body, left him spent and gasping on the floor of the canoe. Uri, whimpering softly, crept to his master's side.

Off to the northeast a haze of light glowed up from the sea. Sometimes the lagoon of an atoll throws up just such a glow. It is the reflection of the lagoon upon the lower sky. Lifting his head, the boy watched it with dulled eyes, uncomprehending at first.

"*Te mori,*" he whispered at last, his voice a thread of awe. "The lagoon-fire."

There came a whir and fury in the sky above, a beat of mighty wings: an albatross, edged with light, circled above the canoe. It swooped low, its gentle, questing eyes turned upon the boy and his dog. Then the bird lifted in its effortless flight, flew straight ahead and vanished into the lagoon-fire. And then Mafatu knew. Hikueru, his homeland, lay ahead. Kivi. . . .

A strangled cry broke from the boy. He shut his eyes tight and there was a taste of salt, wet upon his lips.

The crowd assembled upon the beach watched the small canoe slip through the reef-passage. It was a fine canoe, artfully built. The people thought at first that it was empty. Silence gripped them, and a chill of awe touched them like a cold hand. Then they saw a head lift above the gunwale, a thin body struggle to sit upright, clinging to the mid-thwart.

"*Aué te aué!*" The cry went up from the people in a vast sigh. So they might speak if the sea should give up its dead.

But the boy who dropped overside into the shallows and staggered up the beach was flesh and blood, albeit wasted and thin. They saw that a necklace of boar's teeth shone upon his chest; a splendid spear flashed in his hand. Tavana Nui, the Great Chief of Hikueru, went forward to greet the stranger. The brave young figure halted, drew itself upright.

"My father," Mafatu cried thickly, "I have come home."

The Great Chief's face was transformed with joy. This brave figure, so thin and straight, with the fine necklace and the flashing spear and courage blazing from his eyes— his son? The man could only stand and stare and stare, as if he could not believe his senses. And then a small yellow dog pulled himself over the gunwale of the canoe, fell at his master's feet. Uri. . . . Far overhead an albatross caught a light of gold on its wings. Then Tavana Nui turned to his people and cried: "Here is my son come home from the sea. Mafatu, Stout Heart. A brave name for a brave boy!"

Mafatu swayed where he stood. "My father, I . . ."

Tavana Nui caught his son as he fell.

94

It happened many years ago, before the traders and missionaries first came into the South Seas, while the Polynesians were still great in numbers and fierce of heart. But even today the people of Hikueru sing this story in their chants and tell it over the evening fires.